THE CHANGE

GUY ADAMS

First published 2017 by Solaris
an imprint of Rebellion Publishing Ltd,
Riverside House, Osney Mead,
Oxford, OX2 0ES, UK

www.solarisbooks.com

ISBN: 978 1 78108 585 1

10 9 8 7 6 5 4 3 2 1

A CIP catalogue record for this book is available
from the British Library.

Designed & typeset by Rebellion Publishing

Printed in the UK

PARIS
A CITY OF FOOLS

FIRST: DARKNESS. THE rustling of things unseen in the aisles, the creak of ancient seats and ancient bones.

Then a single spotlight falls onto the stage finding a thin young man, his dreadlocked hair glistening in the dust-filled beam of light.

For a moment he looks hesitant. He's reluctant to be here of course, aren't they all? Then, accepting, he begins to speak.

'You want to know?' he says. 'You want to know what brought me here? About the world outside?' He stares into the darkness and his hooded, tired eyes are filled with anger. 'Fine, then I'll tell you.'

Chapter One

'WHERE WERE YOU when it happened?' That's what everyone always wants to know. That's the question everybody asks. Where was I? Where I always was, beneath the ground and beneath your attention.

I've been living on the streets four years, since my twelfth birthday. No, you do not get to ask why (or, at least, you don't get an answer, I suppose I can't stop you asking). You just have to understand, I came here because it was all I could do. It is all any of us could do, that is why we're here, living in the airless bubble of your indifference.

People look at the homeless as if they are expressing a choice. They think we could be elsewhere. They think we brought it on ourselves. I suppose some played a part, their addictions, their illness, robbing them of better alternatives. But even then… Do you ask a crippled man why he doesn't walk? Nobody lives out there because they want to. Whatever brought them here: fear, illness, addiction, poverty—it was something they couldn't control. If you could control your life you wouldn't guide it out into the cold and the dark. You would aim for the sun.

It doesn't matter. You'll think what you want to think. Even now when we're all the same, adrift in a world that hates us. Living side-by-side with the dead.

Of course, this is not new. Paris has always co-existed with the dead. Beneath the streets, beneath the tunnels of the Metro, are kilometres of catacombs that hold the bones of the forgotten. In the old days, when people cared, they tried to keep you out. There were policemen, catching people who thought it was exciting to climb down from their world above. Sometimes they were caught, sometimes they weren't. They were not as clever as we were. They were tourists in the underworld. We knew how to hide, how to turn the blindness of the authorities to our advantage. To most people we were dead anyway, why not live in a necropolis?

Now, some of the bones move again. They are not

dangerous. They mean no harm. They just sit in the shadows and stare out of empty eye sockets. Sometimes they shake. Nobody really knows why. The tongues that could have told us have rotted away. I think I know. I think they are crying, or coming as close to it as they can without their eyes. I think they are remembering what they once were.

There is no point in this. People think the past is where you were safe, I think it's the most dangerous place of all. It can hurt you more than the future.

If any of us really have one.

There are more of us living there since The Change. Once people realised the dead were no danger, the tunnels seemed a safer bet than the streets. It's just as well there is plenty of space.

Not all the new visitors were welcome. Some tried to bring their old rules, their old sense of superiority. They thought they were still better than us. They thought their money and their expensive clothes meant something. We showed them that wasn't true.

The rest have fitted in. They have learned the skills they need to survive. They have become builders, hunters, medics, guards. Some, like Adrien, have become friends.

I need to tell you about Adrien.

Adrien should not have survived. Sometimes, when things are hard, when we are under attack from the things that prey on us down there—safer it may be but that doesn't mean we don't have our fair share of threats, nowhere is completely safe anymore—I see the panic in his eyes and I wonder if maybe it wouldn't have been easier for him if he'd been with his parents that morning. All of them could have looked up into the sky, seen the things that appeared there and broke the world. If he had seen them, as so many did, he would have died like all the rest. It would have been quick, it would have spared him from the world they left behind.

But Adrien was not with his parents. He was in bed. He was asleep.

Adrien was spared a quick death by a virus.

Adrien missed the end of one world and the birth of another.

I found him during one of my food runs. He'd been hiding on a shelf in the supermarket, surrounded by half-eaten food and wrapped in a packing blanket. Adrien is ten years old and I should have left him where I found him. Instead, I brought him back with me. I made him my problem. I have done my best to keep him alive ever since.

I should have known it was impossible. I was bound to let him down sooner or later.

On the day that brought me here, that tore me from the safety of the tunnels and facing you now, I failed him.

Chapter Two

I TOLD YOU there were things that preyed on us in the tunnels. Creatures from above, looking for food. The purple worms that push themselves up through the earth, needing somewhere warm to plant their eggs. The Vampire Shadows that fall across you and drink you dry. Then, of course, The Impressionists.

They appeared a few months ago, hunting in small packs. From a distance, or in silhouette, they look human enough but when you get close you see them for what they really are. Their skin glistens and moves, their bodies ripple. Wherever they go they leave stains, their fingers daubing the tunnels as they feel their way in the dark. They're solid when they want to be, liquid when they don't. They flood over you and suffocate you. The Impressionists, as mad as it sounds, are made entirely from paint.

They have attacked four times now. Leaving drowned victims behind, faces covered in rich colours. They kidnap people, choke them unconscious and carry them away.

After the second attack, a small group followed them, wanting to find out where they came from. We never saw them again.

I always told Adrien that the most important thing to do if he ever saw The Impressionists was to run. Kids never listen do they?

Chapter Three

'I'M HUNGRY.'

'We're all hungry, Adrien. I'll try and bring you something nice.'

I was due to do another food run. The trips were taking us longer and longer as we were forced to move farther through a city that was already heavily raided. Adrien always asked to come, I always said no. It was dangerous enough out there without having to keep an eye on him too.

'I know how to look after myself,' he said, fidgeting with a small knife I'd given him.

'That's not a toy,' I told him, sounding like every parent ever. 'You'll cut yourself. Get a disease.' I snatched it off him, sheathed it and handed it back. 'Put it away in your pocket.'

He did, in that exasperated way kids always do when you tell them off. 'I'm careful,' he said, 'I haven't cut myself yet have I?'

'No,' I admitted, 'so keep it sheathed and in your pocket and let's keep it that way.'

'No point in having a knife if you never use it,' he said, scratching at his straggly blonde hair. He had something irritating his scalp but I didn't know what to do about it. I'd tried to find him some medicated shampoo but most of the chemists were empty and burned out these days.

'You have it hoping you'll never have to use it,' I explained, 'but keep it close in case you do.'

He shrugged. He was feeling embarrassed now. Like a little kid trying to impress his older brother and failing. A miserable feeling. I tried to make it go away.

'You don't want to come with me anyway,' I said, 'not really. It's boring. You're better off here. I wouldn't go if I didn't have to. Tell you what, when I get back, we'll go and play football in the tunnels alright?'

He smiled. 'Alright. I promise not to knock dead people's heads off again.'

He pretended to be sorry about that but I remembered how loudly he'd laughed when the ball went wild and an ancient cadaver lost a foot in height. I'd laughed too.

There's not much comedy in the world now, you take what you can get.

'You'd better not. How would you like it if they pulled yours off, eh?'

I pretended to do just that. He was almost happy again by the time I had to go. Almost.

I left him with Paulette, who liked nothing better than fussing over the kids.

'It's all for them,' she always said, 'everything we do.'

She's always saying stuff like that. As if we're building a future, not just staying alive day to day. I don't see that the kids are going to have much of a world to grow up in but I keep my mouth shut; you soon recognise the people that fight to stay cheerful because the alternative is to go mad. You let them have their false happiness. After all, they've lost everything else.

She ruffled Adrien's hair—he hated it but, like me, knew she was doing it to make herself feel good, not him—and took him over to where the rest of the kids were trying to avoid boredom. We had power down here in the tunnels, thanks to the hard work from Gerard and his team, but it was easily overloaded and the use of it was controlled. The days of dumping your kids in front of games consoles were long gone.

I met up with the rest of my crew in the Larder: Lucille, a woman with punk hair that always seemed to me to be trying too hard. It was as if she was scared of being boring so she used a lot of colour and hairspray to compensate. The result was a boring woman with weird hair. She could handle herself though, however dull her conversation, and was the best fighter of the group. Then there was Antonio, a quiet old man who spent a good deal of his time staring into space. I wondered what he was thinking about; his old life probably, just like the dead in their alcoves. He was our mapmaker and knew the tunnels better than any of us. The last of the team was Michel, who hummed tunes to himself constantly, afraid of silence. He wasn't a popular member of the crew, when you were trying to pass through the streets without being spotted, the last thing you needed was a guy who never shut up. Besides, you spent more time trying to figure out what song he was humming than you did looking where you were going. One day I was going to get myself killed trying to remember the title of a Fadz tune. Michel was the only one of us who had any real potholing experience so we put up with him. Some of the tunnels were lethal and he'd saved our necks a few times, even if he had done it noisily.

The Larder was Chloe's world, she walked up and down the rows, watering and taking soil samples, adding dried nutrients and muttering to herself about the changes in humidity and temperature. It was generally agreed that Chloe preferred the company of her fungi to that of the rest of us. Michel had said as much to her face once.

'Of course I do,' she had replied, 'the fungi gives, you take. I can't survive down here feeding off you can I? At least, not for long…'

Which was true enough and nobody held her attitude against her. Even if they had they'd have kept their mouths shut because without her we'd all have been even hungrier than we were. There were ten food crews like mine but Chloe provided more to eat these days than all of us combined. In the section of the catacombs that she'd made her own, she grew several species of mushroom that supplemented what we found on the streets. It was only a matter of time, she had argued, before we'd stop being able to find anything and, at that point, our only hope if we wanted to avoid cannibalism was that she could cultivate enough down here to fill our plates. Nobody enjoyed eating the stuff, but the alternative was worse so nobody moaned about Chloe.

Her latest project was the installation of UV lamps so

that she might widen the range of what could be grown. A year ago, nobody would have got excited about the prospect of a tomato or a lettuce, now people talked about them in revered tones. People used to get excited about gold or diamonds or oil; one day, I thought, wars will break out over salad ingredients.

'Going out again?' she asked. 'A few more hours wandering the city for the sake of a few tins of beans?'

The fact that our trips are what had brought her the UV lamps was forgotten, as far as she was concerned we were a symptom of the lazy "old ways", a habit that needed to be broken. Didn't stop her eating the chocolate we occasionally found.

'I don't know what Tomas does all day,' Chloe continued, 'considering how little the crews bring him.'

Tomas was the man in charge of the stores. He catalogued everything the food crews brought in and handled its allocation. Whatever Chloe said, he was a busy man.

'Any requests?' asked Lucille, not rising to the bait.

'Several more acres and a portable sun,' Chloe replied, her attention wandering already as she checked the earth beneath her UV amps for sign of life.

Michel raised an eyebrow but didn't reply, just hummed a few bars of an old song.

Chapter Four

YOU WANT TO know how to find us? You think you can track us down? Good luck with that.

There are over two hundred kilometres of tunnels beneath the city. Some of them are flooded. Some of them lead nowhere. The access points are often so narrow you have to force yourself through with someone pulling your hands or pushing your feet. Without a guide, you're likely to end up trapped down there. You'll starve or drown. Please, try and come and find us, it's a great way of getting rid of you.

We probably haven't mapped a third of it. Antonio takes notes, makes sketches, builds coded signs; he's getting there but who knows if he'll survive long enough to finish the job?

Even if some of the tunnels are new to us, there are traces of people who've been there before. People have explored there for years. They painted on the walls, built shrines, sculptures, marked their way with graffiti and piles of trash. Humans mark their territory like dogs, pissing their tags from aerosol cans. Humans will live in anything given the right circumstances. It used to be a playground, now it's a new city. Our city.

We do most of our travelling beneath the ground, coming up into the light only when we're where we want to be. It's safer that way and we've become more comfortable underground. People adapt quickly. We're at home in the dark. We make trips a couple of times a week but every time we step out into the air it takes us a few minutes to acclimatise. That's the dangerous time, the time we're really vulnerable. It's not just the light, though the sunglasses only cut down some of it, it's also the open space. Every time I climb up out of a manhole or a Metro entrance, I feel a sense of sickness, of the world being too damn big. A sky that goes on forever. It's cold in the tunnels but the chill the wind brings is different, like being breathed on by God. I used to like sitting in the sun, walking in the Luxembourg Gardens, now I hate it. It's too exposed, too bright, there's just too much air.

Once we've got used to it we keep to the sides of the buildings, use the cars for cover. It's not just the creatures you have to worry about, it's the people who stayed above. Everyone's a monster these days.

So many of the shops have been raided. You're better off searching the buildings. We find most of our stuff in apartments—tins and dried food left in cupboards. Sometimes there are still people living there in which case we steer clear. Partly because, well, who are we to mess with someone else's belongings? We hadn't got to the point where we were stealing from others. Not yet. The other reason was basic self-preservation. We were once attacked by a family of cannibals in a flat on Saint-Germaine. They'd sharpened their teeth with nail files and the place stank of meat and shit. We only survived because Lucille puts in as much time with a bow and arrow as she does with her hair. Once mummy was skewered, the kids were quick to run.

That trip, pickings were even worse than usual. Over three hours moving from building to building and all we'd found was a box of vacuum-packed bread rolls and several tins of soup.

Finally, Antonio rescued the trip by stumbling on a couple of sealed packets of coffee. It wouldn't go far but at least Tomas would be walking around with a smile on his face for a couple of days.

We made our way back to the closest tunnel access-point.

Just around the corner from the manhole that would lead us back home, we heard the sound of breaking glass and took cover in the entranceway of a shop. We fought when we had to but only an idiot seeks out opportunities to die.

We heard something large making its way along the road. Heavy feet crunching debris as it came in our direction. Its reflection appeared in the windows across the street: a rhinoceros, its head swinging from side to side as it searched for food.

It wasn't the first time we'd come across a wild animal, a number of them had broken free of their confinement at the zoo. Most had been hunted by residents whose interest in exotic wildlife now extended no further than roasting it over a fire. Those left were the animals that put up more of a fight. One of Gerard's electricity team had been attacked by a leopard when fixing power cables; the rest only escaped because the leopard was too hungry to risk losing one meal on the off chance of catching another.

As the rhino drew level with us we could see that it was malnourished and ailing in this new concrete world. Its body twitched as it took faltering steps along the road.

'If we could fit that in our packs,' said Michel, 'we'd return as heroes.'

'I'm not risking my life for meat that could be diseased,' said Antonio. 'Besides, be sensible, even if we could kill it, we'd have to butcher it in the middle of the street, cutting off as much as we could carry. We'd be too exposed.'

I didn't fancy carrying a bleeding chunk of rhino on my back and said as much. Once, the mere thought of killing another animal would have been something I couldn't imagine doing. I wasn't a vegetarian but nor had I ever been hungry enough to end a life, and, living rough, I'd been hungrier than most. Post-Change such moral viewpoints had shifted; we'd have happily killed the thing if it had been possible to take the carcass back with us. We'd caught a few rabbits, even rats, but some of the tunnels were so narrow that anything bigger would be impossible to carry. Besides, as Antonio had said, the rhino didn't look healthy. It was swaying from side to side, its feet dragging on the road. It looked like an old man dancing, ancient hips struggling to capture a rhythm they remembered but could no longer maintain.

As we watched, it halted, its head shaking as if trying to dislodge something from one of its stubby ears. Then it turned slightly and it was Lucille who first realised what was happening.

'It knows we're here,' she said. 'We need to move.'

'And get caught in the open?' asked Michel.

'Better that than boxed in here,' she replied, stepping slowly towards the sidewalk. 'Move as gently as possible. If it thinks we're a threat it'll definitely charge.'

We followed her, inching our way out onto the street. The rhino watched as we moved away, backs pressed against the shop windows.

'You think it's going to attack?' asked Michel, his voice shaking.

'Keep talking and maybe we'll find out,' she replied. 'It doesn't want to eat us but who knows its state of mind? Look at it.'

We hadn't taken our eyes off it. It hadn't stopped staring at us either. Its small black eye, buried at the centre of the rough, skin circles on its face, was fixed on us.

It came to a decision, lifting its head into the air, its mouth opened and the most awful noise erupted from it. This was no natural call, this was the reality infection caused by The Change. Earlier, we'd thought something was breaking windows but that sound, the shattering of glass, was the rhino's voice. It turned towards us and began to charge.

'Split up!' Lucille said, her voice barely raised as she ran off in a diagonal, aiming for the other side of the street.

We did as she said, all of us except Antonio. He just stood there, staring at the rhino as it came towards him. It wasn't fast, at least, not as fast as it once would have been, but if he didn't move he'd only have seconds to live.

Michel began yelling at the top of his voice, running towards the animal. Distracted, it halted a couple of metres from Antonio and turned towards Michel.

As it charged towards a new target, I ran and grabbed Antonio, dragging him away.

Michel was running as fast as he could, weaving and looking for cover as the rhino closed in on him. Just as it was almost on top of him, he rolled to one side and it continued on, unable to stop itself from crashing into a parked car. There was a crunch of metal and its head vanished inside the car's cabin. Michel was on his feet and running, just behind the rest of us, as we aimed for the manhole cover and safety.

Behind us the rhino fought to free itself from the chassis of the car but, confused and weak, it could do little more than shake the car from side to side.

I watched it as Lucille lifted the manhole and the rest of them climbed down one by one.

'Come on Loic,' said Lucille, when we were the last two on the street.

The rhino had given up now, its back legs shaking and twitching.

'It would have been amazing once,' I said, 'beautiful.'

'Not any more,' she said, 'now it's as ugly as the rest of us.'

BACK BELOW GROUND, Antonio had regained control of himself.

'Sorry,' he said, 'I'm so sorry.' He looked at Michel. 'You risked your life for me.'

'Nobody knows these tunnels better than you,' Michel said, 'if you'd died we'd probably never have got back.'

Humming again, he gestured for Antonio to lead the way and we followed him towards home.

Chapter Five

IT WAS AN hour or so before we made it back and we were greeted not by the usual excited questions as to what we'd found but a general panic. In our absence, The Impressionists had attacked again. Only three of them but that was more than enough to cause trouble.

One of them had been captured. We were all shocked to hear this; given their nature it was all but impossible to fight them let alone restrain them.

'After the last time,' said Henri, the man who fancied himself as head of security, 'I got to thinking about ways we could deal with them.'

Henri had been in the army, though not for a few years. Whenever anyone asked him why he'd left he would give a different answer, usually hinting at some terrible injustice or moral decision that forced his hand. Most of us suspected he'd got booted out and just didn't want to admit it. If he'd really pulled off what he'd claimed then he'd be treated like royalty for months to come.

He led us into one of the main access passages, a route The Impressionists had used twice before.

'We put a watch in place,' he said, 'not that it does much good, we can't stop them getting in, but at least we now have warning.'

To one side of the tunnel was a large object covered by a tarpaulin.

'I also managed to rig this up,' he said uncovering it.

Underneath there was a large perspex container, taller than a man and twice my width.

'Used for storing grain,' he said, 'rigged a vacuum pump to the top. When the things came in two of my boys attacked one of them with the vacuum, sucked it right up!'

Inside the container, the creature wasn't making much effort to appear human. Beyond the basic outline of a head and torso it was little more than a pillar of thick paint, swaying from side to side like a cobra.

'It let you?' asked Michel.

'Didn't have much choice did it?' said Henri. 'Too quick for it.'

Michel's face mirrored the rest of our thoughts. In our experience The Impressionists could become solid with no more than a thought. Why hadn't it just done so the minute Henri's men had tried to suck it into the container?

'I wouldn't stand too close to it if I were you,' said Lucille, putting her hand on my shoulder.

'You worry too much!' said Henri, clearly angry that we weren't giving him the appreciation he felt he deserved. 'It's trapped, this thing's solid.' He banged on the side of the perspex tube and the creature inside turned towards him.

'What you looking at, eh?' Henri laughed.

It threw itself at the side of the container, spraying against the clear perspex in a swirl of colour. Henri fell backwards in panic. As the paint dripped down the inside of the canister it momentarily took on the form of a smiling face, white and red-lipped like a clown.

Henri was quick to get back on his feet, terrified of looking weak in front of the rest of us.

'Showing off won't help you,' he said to the creature in the canister. 'You're ours now. Your friends left you. So maybe you should try being a bit more cooperative, eh? If you answer a few of our questions maybe we won't hurt you too badly.'

Antonio scratched his head, turning his back towards the container. 'Surely that rather depends on two things: it being able to communicate and our being able to hurt it?'

'Going to pump some acetone in there,' said Henri, 'see how it likes that.'

He held up a length of hosing that was connected to the top of the canister. Lucille snatched at it but he pushed her back. 'Careful! Open the valve on that and it'll have a way out.'

Lucille was shaking her head. 'As if we didn't have enough to worry about you've now built a time bomb in our home.'

Henri was clearly furious. He'd expected praise and he'd received criticism. He turned his backs on us and began tugging the tarpaulin back in place.

'You just carry on wasting your days out there and leave the rest of us to get on with the real work,' he said.

I got one final glimpse of the creature before the tarpaulin covered it completely. It had reformed into a more human shape and appeared to be waving at us.

Chapter Six

AT THE STORES, we unpacked the little we'd found.

Tomas couldn't pretend to be impressed at the soup and bread but, as predicted, the coffee got a better reaction.

'I'll add this to the rest,' he said, 'a bit more and we'll have enough for everyone to have a cup.'

He was fair like that, stockpiling the rarer items like coffee, chocolate and alcohol so it could be evenly distributed.

'Any of the other teams back yet?' Michel asked

'Aimée and Marianne got back half an hour ago,' Tomas said, taking off his glasses and sighing in despair at the filthiness of the lenses. 'Can't keep anything clean down here,' he moaned, rubbing at the lenses with his sweatshirt. 'They did ok. Italian restaurant with several boxes of dried pasta. Marianne found a tray of tinned pears too.'

'A perfect combination,' said Lucille. 'I know what we'll be eating tomorrow evening.'

Tomas shook his head. 'Tomorrow Chloe is unveiling some new mycoprotein blend she's come up with in the vats. No doubt it'll taste like all the others. Who knew the end of the world would turn us all into vegetarians? I've given her as many spices as I could to try and pep it up a bit.'

'Did The Impressionists cause much trouble?' asked Antonio.

Tomas shrugged. 'The usual. I don't think there were any actual casualties this time, most people just hide and wait for them to leave. I suppose there's not much else to do but I don't like it. They took a couple of kids with them.'

'Kids?' I asked, feeling panicked.

Tomas nodded. 'I don't know who, I'm afraid. I'm out of the loop down here, nobody keeps me informed. Twice now we've been attacked without me knowing about it until the panic was over.'

I said my goodbyes to the rest of the crew and ran

through the tunnels on the hunt for Paulette. I was trying to convince myself that the odds of Adrien being one of the missing were slim. There were a fair number of kids down here after all. Of course, wishing that made me feel guilty, but there's so much death now you'd go mad if you didn't focus on your own.

Paulette was in her chamber, doing her best to reassure a couple of the younger kids that the trouble was over. She had her best happy face in place but I could see from her puffy eyes that it was a mask, a bit of theatre to keep the kids from panicking. As soon as she looked up and saw me it all but fell apart.

'Oh Loic,' she said, 'I'm so sorry. I tried to protect him but he...' She began to cry. 'So brave. He tried to lead them away from the rest of the children. He was such an amazing boy...'

I didn't want to hear what he 'was' anymore so I left.

Chapter Seven

I KNOW. IT was stupid. I shouldn't have got attached. He was just some kid. He shouldn't have been my problem. I had enough other things to deal with. It's not like I could have taken him on the food run. He should have been safer here. Yes. That's what it should have been. Safer.

I went back to the creature Henri had captured.

Henri wasn't there but he'd left one of his people, Laure, on guard. She was standing well back, very sensible, probably wondering exactly what she was supposed to do if the thing broke free.

'I want to talk to it,' I told her, walking up to the canister and tugging the tarpaulin aside.

'I'm not sure that's…' She stopped talking and looked

around for someone else she could call on. She could see that I wasn't going to take no for an answer and it would take more than words to keep me from what I wanted.

I stared at the creature in the tank. It was little more than a mound of alternating colours now, purple to red, red to blue, blue to an autumn brown.

'Where do you take them?' I asked it. 'The people you kidnap. Where do you go?'

It pulsed slightly. Could it understand me? I thought of the smiling face it had presented to Henri. Was that the sarcastic jibe it had appeared to be or just coincidence? How did these things think?

'Answer me!' I shouted, banging on the perspex. 'Where do you take them?'

It reformed into a human shape; after a moment I realised it was copying me, my hair as liquid spikes, colour matching the rest of me, my clothes, the tone of my skin.

It extended a finger to the perspex and a splatter of paint erupted from its tip. The paint formed words on the perspex, reversed so that I could read them: *Only one way to find out.*

'Oi!' Henri had returned. 'What are you doing? Keep back from there.'

The words began to run, swirling around and reforming into new ones: *How badly do you want to know?*

Could we torture it like Henri thought? I doubted it. I think it would stay as long as it wanted to. The minute it had a chance to escape it would do so, taking one more of us along with it. In the meantime it watched and learned; a spy, curious rather than scared.

'Come on,' said Henri, grabbing my arm. 'I told you to keep back.'

I nodded at the creature. 'I want to know,' I said.

I pulled myself free from Henri and grabbed the hose that hung from the top of the canister. The valve at the end had a circular tap fixed to it, I turned it, much to Henri's disgust.

'What are you playing at, you idiot?'

He made to pull the hose out of my hand but I shoved him backwards and flung the hose away from both of us. It thickened as the creature hurled itself to the top of the canister and began to force itself free.

'Stupid kid!' Henri shouted, scrabbling in the dirt for the end of the hose, desperate to close it off. I held him back.

'Stay out of the way,' I told him, 'or it'll go for you too.'

The creature spilled from the hose, a widening circle of thick paint. From its centre a pillar rose up that reformed into a human shape.

'What should we do?' asked Laure but Henri was already running past her.

'Nothing we can do!' he shouted. 'Just try and keep out of its way.'

But I knew it wasn't going to attack them, why should it? It had what it wanted.

It extended a slick hand towards me and I took a step back. 'No,' I said. 'No need to choke me. I'm going willingly aren't I? Take me where you take the others.'

Chapter Eight

WE WERE FOLLOWED to begin with. Henri, Laure and others all begging me to turn back. But what would have been the point of that? The Impressionist had to take someone, that someone was me. I either walked there of my own free will or it would choke the consciousness out of me and carry me.

But why go at all?

I couldn't think of any other way of finding out where The Impressionists went.

Adrien. He had been quiet to begin with, but I could understand that. I'd been quiet when I'd first found myself on the streets. When you're young you learn quickly to make yourself invisible if you feel threatened. It's nature. You look around you at the world you find yourself in, hostile and unknowable, an alien planet you can never imagine fitting in to, and you just shut up. You shrink, you hunch yourself, you give off a wave of invisibility. It's what every kid does when they have a parent that hits them, a bully who beats them in the schoolyard, a gang that calls them names. They escape inside and disappear. Adrien had that. I'd had it too.

I know what you're thinking. You're thinking I only wanted to protect him because he reminded me of myself. Well, you may be that self-obsessed but I just sympathised, ok? I understood and wanted to give him something better.

Sometimes you just take stupid risks to help the people in life you care about.

After a while with me he'd laughed more. He'd talked more. He'd come out of hiding.

At night he'd tell me stories about his old life, about his folks or things that had happened to him at school. Ok, so maybe if he'd been older I'd have told him how none of that stuff mattered anymore, that the past is wiped away the minute it's over, but he wasn't. He needed that grounding. He needed to think that there was still a normal out there to be found again one day. Sooner or later he'd realise it had vanished for good but that would be something he'd discover for himself, not have hammered into him by me. I guess we'd all get along better if we let people find their own way, we so rarely do.

I would sit and listen to him talk and I'd find a little piece of normal for myself. Yeah, at the same time I'd be panicking, reminding myself that all I was doing was giving myself one more problem to deal with, one more way to get hurt, but mostly those thoughts came when he wasn't around. When he was there I just let it be.

Whether Adrien should have been my responsibility or not didn't matter. He was, so I needed to try to look after him. Now that meant doing something stupid in case he could still be helped. Probably I'd be too late, but I would have tried. What's anything worth these days without a few principles? Survival? Yeah, well, that's all well and good but unless you do something with your life beyond your next breath, your next meal, what's it all for? We were all walking dead, something was likely to kill us sooner or later, accept that and you might as well die having tried to do something decent, don't you think?

No, of course, you wouldn't think that. But that's because you've never done a decent thing in your lives.

You were worthless before The Change and you're worthless now. I don't know why I bother trying to explain it to you. If you were a decent human being you wouldn't need it explaining in the first place.

After a while, the others gave up and I walked with the creature alone, its skin shimmering in the torches and halogen lamps we'd strung up along the tunnels. Was I scared? Of course I was. Chances were I was walking to my death.

I guess I was. Though not quite in the way I imagined then.

Chapter Nine

BY THE TIME we were back in the open air—and no, I'm still not going to tell you where we came out, I'm not stupid and you're getting this story on my terms, deal with it—the sun was getting low.

The creature had made no attempt to communicate with me while we'd been in the tunnels, it had just moved along in front of me, a slight sloshing sound echoing off the walls with each step it took.

Now, in the open air, it stretched itself out, long liquid limbs raised towards the sky as if enjoying the heat of the sun. It still held a roughly human shape, not bothering with features but retaining a torso, limbs and head.

Tendrils sprouted from the end of its arm-like limbs and, blossoming from each like petals on branches formed a letter. *Love the light,* it said. *Light brings clarity.*

I didn't share the opinion, and I didn't care what it loved. 'Let's just get on with it,' I said, 'we have places to go.'

The letters changed. *No rush. You will see.*

'Are you telling me that the kids you took are already dead?'

No. Nothing changes today.

It began to move again and I noticed it was quicker in the light, its skin shimmering and changing colour as the late afternoon sun hit it. It thrived up here, no wonder it *loved the light.*

We joined the Rue Montmartre, heading south towards the river. The shops and cafés were deserted of course, empty, raided buildings. One small coffee table was a mass of fungal growth, the remains of a pair of lunches having been left to grow wild. Graffiti tags covered old stone, turning it into veined cheese, windows stood shattered and furniture had been cleared out into the street. Nature had taken over: a pile of wooden chairs had become the heart of a thriving vine, its green branches weaving through the wood. A solitary tendril reached for the sky with nowhere left to climb to.

Some would mourn the death of the city, the ancient buildings, centuries of history, now a rotting carcass. Personally, the city had never done me any favours, I hadn't drunk coffee in these cafés—though I'd earned a few euros from those that had—I hadn't browsed these shops. This had been someone else's word and decay was welcome to it. Besides, if history has told us anything it's that something else will come one day. Cities of the future would dig out archeological remains of this world and shove it in their museums. Nothing lasts forever, especially not civilisations.

The creature paused outside the shell of a small art gallery, its indistinct head twitching slightly as if it sensed something. Then a tendril of paint burst out from its chest, shooting into the air. It wrapped itself around a swooping pigeon, like the darting tongue of a lizard, pulling the flapping bird back into its body where the paint closed over its squawking head. Letters appeared from the creature's shoulders. *Hungry*, it explained.

'Rather the bird than me,' I said.

Too big, it replied. *Not digest.*

We continued towards the river, in the direction of the Louvre. I guessed that was probably where we were going, if there was anywhere paintings would choose to live it was the Louvre.

At one point I noticed we were being watched from the windows above—a group of survivors, dressed in tatty evening clothes, wild hair crammed into top hats, strings of pearls slung around grimy necks. One of them raised a champagne glass at me and smiled a rotten smile. Even when the world was over the party carried on for some.

When we reached the Louvre other Impressionists were converging on the building just as we were. Mosts were carrying objects: vases, paintings, sculptures. One was even dragging a grand piano behind it.

'You like a lot of stuff,' I said.

It turned to me, its face morphing into a big pair of smiling lips. From out of the lips popped a word at a time: *Museum. Need. Stuff. We. Collect. Stuff.*

'Including people?'

In. Beginning. Then. Realised. Full. Set. Not. Fit. Now. For. Trade.

'Trade? With who?'

Tomorrow.

It took hold of my arm and dragged me through the gardens towards the pyramid entrance. Several Impressionists were climbing on the glass, apparently entertaining one another by adopting different shapes. One turned itself into the French flag, rippling in a pretend wind, another mimicked an explosion in torrents of orange and grey.

Inside, the large corridors were filled with the sound of shifting and construction.

The original displays had been augmented by The Impressionists' scavenging. Ancient sculptures stood side by side with immaculately placed relics of the world pre-Change. There was everything from televisions to tins of food, all mounted and displayed as if they were vitally important works of art.

A long line of alcoves contained people, set in various poses as if to mimic the life they'd once had. A man in a business suit lifted his briefcase up to show passers-by; a woman in a pilot's uniform placed a finger to her disconnected earpiece as if receiving orders from the flight tower; a small child stared up at a static red balloon hovering just above her head. Their skin shone as if they'd been varnished, but I knew they must have been living human beings once. As I passed, their eyes followed me along the corridor and I realised the horrible truth: they were living still, frozen in place but aware of the world around them.

The creature led me to the painting gallery. The frames showed blank canvases and I realised this was where The Impressionists had come from; ancient paint, somehow brought to life and given shapes and desires of their own. At the far end of the gallery a group of people were tied up with the rope that would have been used to form barriers, keeping tourists from touching the displays.

I searched their faces and finally found the one I was looking for.

'Adrien!' He looked up and the hope on his face at seeing me almost made the whole thing worthwhile. I hoped we would both live long enough to deserve it.

'Loic! They got you too!'

'I came looking for you,' I told him, grabbing him in my arms and accepting a crushing hug.

I saw above him that not all the paintings had vacated their frames. From inside her bulletproof case, the Mona Lisa stared down at us with her usual ambivalence.

The Impressionist that had brought me here stared at her and a pair of words appeared above its head: *Grumpy cow.*

Then he tied me up next to Adrien and left.

Chapter Ten

'THIS IS WHY you should have let me come on the food hunt,' said Adrien. 'If you had we'd both be sat in the tunnels now.'

He smiled to show he was making a joke (though, if we got out of there I knew he would use it as ammunition to get his own way forever).

It seemed that, just by being with him, I had turned the scary situation into one that wasn't worth worrying about. I didn't like the fact that he had such blind faith in me but it was better than him panicking.

'You would probably have got trodden on by a rhinoceros,' I told him. 'Which would have hurt a lot more than getting picked on by paint people.'

There were about twenty of us in all, of varying ages.

Other than Gabi, the other child they'd taken from the tunnels, I didn't recognise anyone, they had all been taken from other groups around the city.

'How are you doing Gabi?' I asked her. She was about eight years old and prone to tantrums. Nobody blamed her, rage was a symptom of the new world.

'I've been looking after her,' said Adrien, 'haven't I Gabi?'

She looked at him, smiled and nodded. Gabi wasn't much of a talker unless she was screaming at the top of her voice.

'I always help Paulette,' said Adrien, adopting that sort of grown-up pretence that some kids can have. 'I'm good at looking after kids.'

'Yes you are,' I told him. *Better than me, probably*, I thought.

'So,' he leaned in and adopted a pinched, "let's keep this secret, ok?" face, 'when are we going to escape?'

Which was a good question. It wasn't the ropes that worried me, they were well-tied but they were shiny and slipped easily, no doubt we could work ourselves free if we helped each other out. The problem was always going to be what we did next. How were we supposed to walk through the Louvre without being seen? We knew how dangerous only a couple of The Impressionists could be and I couldn't see how we were going to get past a whole army of them.

I decided that our best bet was probably to wait. Tomorrow we were to be traded with someone, maybe then, possibly out in the open, we'd have our chance to make a break for it.

I told Adrien this and he pulled a disappointed face. 'You mean we have to stay the night?'

'Yeah,' I replied, 'we have to stay the night.'

'Probably our last night on earth,' said a man next to us. 'If you really think you're going to escape you're kidding yourselves.'

I gave him an angry stare. He might be right but there was no need to say it in front of the kids. The woman next to him obviously agreed. 'Shut up Jean,' she said, 'this is bad enough without your miserable whining.'

She was in her late forties, head shaved, with a tattoo of a rose on her bare scalp. She patted Adrien's hand. 'Don't listen to him,' she said, 'he's always moaning.'

The man opened his mouth to speak again but then looked at Gabi who was staring up at him, the look on her face suggesting that the next thing he said would be the most important thing she'd ever hear. He sighed.

'Yeah, sorry,' he rolled his eyes, 'just had a bit of a bad day, you know?'

Gabi seemed partially satisfied and she went back to staring at her hands.

Adrien was grinning. 'I know we'll be alright,' he said. 'Loic will sort it, he's brilliant at sorting things.'

The woman smiled but the man couldn't quite hide his sneer. 'Good for Loic,' he said. 'I'll remember to look to him when the trouble starts.'

I didn't argue. How could I? It's not like I could insist Adrien was right.

I just hoped that tomorrow an opportunity would present itself.

Chapter Eleven

It wasn't a comfortable night; it was bad enough having to sleep on the floor tied to one another but when the statuary started screaming we really knew we were in for a rough time. I had been disturbed by the captured citizens displayed as exhibits downstairs and it seemed their fate was somehow shared by all the classical statues. Cold, marble voices moaned about their entrapment, about aches and pains they couldn't stretch, itches they couldn't scratch. Every statue in the place had a nervous breakdown throughout the hours of darkness. By the time it was morning, I knew how they felt.

As the first light of dawn came, silence fell, by which time it was far too late to make use of it.

Adrien and Gabi had both slept a little, leaning on me,

so at least they would have some energy for whatever the day might bring.

The Impressionists came for us at about eight o'clock. There were ten of them, all adopting different shapes: some squat and fat, some thin and spindly, some all hard angles and jutting points, some like liquid clouds.

One of them stepped forward and presented words from his flat palms.

Get. Up. Trade. Now.

We did as we were told, relieved to be able to move.

They marched us back through the gallery. They'd been busy overnight installing more exhibits. There was now part of an old Citroën hanging from the roof, slung nose-down as if frozen just before driving into the floor at speed. A bank of microwave ovens hummed and glowed, their little glass plates revolving and clattering for no culinary reason. A pile of bicycles, somehow interlinked—spoke through spoke, crossbar through crossbar—towered towards the ceiling, wheels spinning, bells jangling. The Impressionists seemed determined to fill every inch of the place.

Outside, a procession of Impressionists bringing new exhibits filed past us as we walked beneath the Arc du Triumph du Carrousel and into the Tuileries Garden.

The gardens were overgrown with nobody to tend them, the grass thick and long, the bushes and shrubs blending into one another, all semblance of design lost.

As we walked down the Allée Centrale I became aware of a crackling sound and kept catching a glimpse of something bright orange out of the corner of my eye.

The Impressionist in front didn't turn around but words sprouted from his head.

Ignore. Historical. Concepts. it suggested.

But this was hard to do once they emerged from hiding. There were four of them, creaking ancient mannequins that perpetually burned, the clothes they had once worn now reduced to dark, ash shadows on their fabric bodies.

'There's no point in praying,' said one, 'nobody's listening.'

'He's Atheism,' said another, 'so he would say that. Personally I think you may as well give it a shot, anything that might help you get ahead in life, eh?'

'Shut up Ambition,' said the third, 'it's me they should be listening to. Not that I want to speak to them anyway, they're not important are they? Nobody's important but me.'

'That's Egoism,' said the last one, 'he is egotistical. Which means he only thinks about himself. Not others.

Just him. Always. I am False Simplicity. Which is a very confusing concept when you think about it, which I'd rather not.'

'We're Robespierre's children,' said Atheism. 'He burned us before the crowds when he was trying to impress. He didn't like us very much.'

'Which was funny really,' said Ambition, 'because we were quite like him in some ways.'

'Let's not get too philosophical,' said False Simplicity. 'These people may be marching to their deaths, the last thing they need is to get all confused. Just concentrate on the road ahead,' it suggested, 'let the more complex things work themselves out on their own.'

'They don't affect me anyway,' said Egoism. 'I'm above all that sort of thing.'

'How did you do it?' Ambition asked. 'Lend a fellow concept a hand.'

'I can't even hear you,' Egoism replied. 'You're dead to me.'

'Just like God,' said Atheism. 'Didn't stop him being popular.'

A couple of Impressionists peeled away from the procession, their hands morphing into large paddles as they shooed the burning figures away.

World. Gone. Mad. announced another, the words bursting from his back like wings.

None of us argued with that.

The garden opened up into the Grand Carré. In the centre was a large octagonal pond. In the pond a selection of verdigris nymphs frolicked. As we walked past, one swam to the edge and eyed us appreciatively. 'Morning sexy,' she said.

'Which one are you talking to?' asked another, splashing water on her smooth, unlined features.

'All of them, of course,' the first nymph replied.

Do. Not. Be. Seduced. suggested the leading Impressionist. *Lovers. Will. Be. Crushed.*

'But what a way to go!' the nymph laughed and threw herself back into the water with a splash and clang.

Through the tall grass to our right a bronze crocodile appeared, its jaws stretched wide.

There was a ripple of panic through the crowd but then another bronze creature appeared: a lion, jumping on the crocodile's back and pinning it to the ground.

'Quickly!' it roared. 'I won't be able to hold it down forever.'

'You've managed for nigh on a hundred fifty years, love,' joked one of the nymphs, 'I doubt you'll struggle now.'

We walked past, aiming for the Place de la Concorde beyond the garden.

In the distance, the Eiffel Tower stretched itself like someone waking from a long sleep. Even from here we could hear the creaking of girders. Suddenly, it bent forward, stabbing at the ground. When it stood upright again we could see the tiny silhouette of someone impaled on the aerial at its tip. There was a creak of metal and the summit opened briefly, like the mouth of a wading bird, to swallow its human prey.

Even the buildings had teeth post-Change.

Chapter Twelve

WE ENTERED THE Place de la Concorde, the open space filled with the shimmering figures of ghosts.

You see this sort of thing in some places. The Change has made lots of weird things happen on the streets but always, the root of it, the logic—if you can ever call it that—is based on the history of the place. It's the geography that's key, the weird creation of The Impressionists from The Louvre, the attacking tower, the dead in the catacombs. Sometimes places kick up ghosts. They're intangible, misty, like projected film of the people that once existed there. In the case of the Place de la Concorde it was the bloodthirsty crowds that had gathered during the Revolution, all wanting to see noble blood spilled by the guillotine. They showed no sign of seeing us—the ghosts never did—and The Impressionists just walked right through them, the ghosts bursting and reforming as the creatures collided with them.

Beyond the ghosts should have been the obelisk, rising up at the centre of the square. It was gone, replaced by a new structure, just as tall, but far wider and alive. It was a guillotine, built from old, dark wood that creaked like an old sailing ship as it flexed in excitement. Rising up and down between the vertical runners was the blade, a rusty thing, its edge jagged like human teeth. It moved up slowly then slammed down, eager to chew on human throats.

Surrounding the guillotine were sat four hooded figures. They were twice the size of a normal human, thin, grey fingers poking out of the sleeves of their robes. The nails on those fingers tapered into long needles that clattered together as they knitted with lengths of dripping wool. As we got closer I began to suspect that it wasn't wool at all, but the glistening innards of the victims they called to their mistress the guillotine.

Dotted around this awful group were pillars standing at shoulder height. On the tops of the pillars sat severed heads, rolling their eyes and chattering to one another.

'Here come some more for Madame Loisette,' one said, 'she's so hungry today, so impatient to slice and chew and sever.'

'They don't look like nobles,' said another, squinting at us, his face pinched and disapproving, 'they look like commoners if you ask me, dirty little peasants.'

'They execute just about anyone these days,' said another, 'it's awfully insulting.'

The leading Impressionist halted and raised its hands so that words could appear from them.

Where. Exhibits? it asked.

One of the knitting figures stopped working, slipped the wet garment from its nails onto the stone floor where it fell with a slap. It got to its feet and beckoned with a sharp finger. From the other side of the square, a wooden cart rolled forward. There was nobody pulling it, its wheels rattled under their own steam. It was the kind of thing that prisoners would have once been carried in, now it contained a pile of junk. I could see a satellite dish, a small tricycle, a display of plastic flowers. The Impressionists quivered with what I guessed was excitement as it drew closer.

Most. Acceptable! announced the creature that was doing all the talking. *We. Trade!*

'Right,' said the man who had been moaning the night before, 'if you've got a plan now would be a good time.' He sneered. 'But you haven't have you? We'll just have to have our heads cut off.'

'If it was good enough for me...' said one of the severed heads.

I turned to Adrien and whispered. 'You got your knife?'

He nodded.

'Then start cutting the ropes so we can run.'

'What good will that do?' the man asked as we were tugged towards the guillotine. 'They'll soon grab us back won't they? You can't outrun them, I tried. They shoot their long arms at you and snatch you back.

'Excuse me?' I called to the Impressionist who seemed to be in charge, the one that had been doing all the 'talking'. I did my best to move away from Adrien slightly so I wasn't drawing attention to him.

The creature turned to face me. *What?* it asked, the word bursting in a spray of bright yellow from its mouth.

'Well, I can see that you're trying to collect all the really important things for the museum,' I said, 'but you haven't got the really good stuff have you? The really amazing things.'

Its skin rippled with red, I wondered if this meant it was angry. Each word spurted aggressively from its chest. *What. Amazing. Things?!?*

'The really rare stuff, you know, the iconic, breathtaking things.' I looked towards the guillotine. 'Like that for example. A grotesque guillotine, evoking an entire period of our history, an emblem of a political movement that changed our country forever. It should definitely be in the museum don't you think? It's essential. Breathtaking. I feel moved to tears just looking at it.'

It turned to look at the guillotine.

'They won't stand for that,' said one of the severed heads. 'Madame Loisette is the boss around here, La Tricoteuse are just her feeders. There may be only four of them but you watch, they'll tear you apart before you so much as lay a finger on her.'

'There's only four of them?' I asked.

'More than enough,' it replied, nodding so vigorously it rolled forward and landed on the floor with the popping of a broken nose.

'Only four,' I said to The Impressionist. 'That's limited edition isn't it? Extremely rare. Much rarer than all the stuff in the cart. Of course, you could take that as well couldn't you? It's not like they could stop you is it?'

Limited. The Impressionist said. The word appearing in a cloud-like thought bubble above its head. *Precious and iconic.*

'Absolutely,' I agreed, 'your museum isn't going to be up to much without them is it?'

I turned to look at Adrien, his hands were free now and the others were passing the knife around, cutting the rope.

All four of La Tricoteuses were getting to their feet, sensing the trouble that was brewing.

The guillotine, Madame Loisette, slammed her blade up and down with renewed energy.

'She's getting angry now,' said another of the heads. 'It's alright for us, we don't have any necks to worry about but I'd be fair terrified if I were you, things are going to get nasty any moment.'

The Impressionist I had talked to, turned to its fellows and one massive word erupted from its body, hanging over its shoulders and head. *COLLECT.*

The chaos was immediate, The Impressionists moved quicker than I had even seen them move before, their bodies losing cohesion as they flung themselves towards the guillotine and the attendant Tricoteuses. You know when you sling water out of a bucket? The way it forms a jagged rectangle that flies through the air, momentum keeping it together for a few seconds? It was just like that except that at the moment gravity normally beats momentum and the shape falls apart, they reformed into a more human shape, landing on the needle-fingered hags and tearing at them with liquid hands.

I reached out my hands to the person now holding the knife. Once the rope had been cut a few times it all began to fall apart and most of us could just pull ourselves free, trying not to think about the violence erupting all around us.

'I knew you'd do it!' said Adrien as I grabbed his hand.

'All I've done so far is cause a fight,' I told him, looking around for Gabi. Everyone was running in separate directions and she was knocked to the ground in the panic.

'Careful!' I shouted as someone nearly trampled her.

I grabbed her hand and yanked her upright. She cried out as I pulled her arm but I couldn't worry about being gentle. Who knew how long this distraction would last?

'Come on!' I said, half carrying, half pulling them in the direction of the road.

The Tricoteuses were wailing, though in anger or pain it was hard to tell, I turned to see one of them, her fingers a blur of movement as she knitted the fabric of one of The Impressionists into a new shape, a net of colour that thrashed and fought to release itself from the shape she had woven it into. Why didn't it just liquefy? Did these other beasts have power over them?

I realised I was wasting time trying to decide who was going to win. It was no benefit to me either way, the best result would be that they killed each other and knocked over that hungry guillotine while they were at it.

The blade was sending splinters into the air now, driven mad with bloodlust at the fighting.

'You've driven her mad!' screamed one of the heads as we ran past. 'She won't be happy until she's taken the heads of the entire city.'

I scooped Gabi into my arms so we could move quicker, Adrien was quick on his feet but Gabi must have been hurt in the scuffle and was limping badly.

Behind us, I heard the sound of the guillotine scaffold toppling, whether because of attack or through its own self-destructive slicing I didn't know.

We ran up Rue Royale, cutting off onto Saint Honoré and then Cambon, not once looking back, in case the winners of the battle were in pursuit.

Chapter Thirteen

FINALLY, ACROSS THE street from the Olympia theatre, still advertising a gala night of music as if it were the most important thing in the world, we stopped running and checked to see if we'd been followed. There was no sign of anyone, not the Impressionists, the Tricoteuses or, for that matter, any of the other people that had been brought for sacrifice to the hungry guillotine.

'My ankle,' said Gabi, 'they stood on it.'

'Let me have a look,' suggested Adrien, as if he had all the medical training she might need.

'I'll do it,' I said, carrying on quickly as I could already see the look of disappointment growing on his face. He didn't like me suggesting he wasn't capable of anything. Always so eager to prove himself. Had I been like that?

I'd probably been too busy watching out for myself around the house, hiding from Uncle Jean. 'You take a look up the street, not far, just enough to make sure the coast's clear, we don't want something creeping up on us.'

He nodded and jogged a little way up the road.

'Stay where I can see you!' I called. 'Just in case.'

He rolled his eyes at that but I didn't care, the last thing I needed was for him to get snatched by something, I'd only just got him back.

I looked at Gabi's ankle. It was puffy and turning red. I roughed up a bandage using her socks, tying it as tightly as possible and then told her she would be getting a piggy-back ride for the rest of the day. That seemed an exciting enough prospect that she forgot about how much her ankle was hurting for a few minutes.

Adrien was stood a little way up the street so, lifting Gabi onto my shoulders, I walked up to join him.

'Where's the closest way back?' he asked.

I told him, but obviously, I'm not telling you. Suffice to say it was a longer walk than I would have liked. Without Antonio I didn't want to risk getting lost, so we'd have to go underground at a familiar spot that I knew I could lead us home from. That would take some walking.

'Well,' he said, 'if you get tired carrying Gabi I can always take over.'

'I'll hold you to that.'

We walked up the street a short way, Adrien doing his very best to act as if this was all in a day's work. I knew him well enough to see the nervousness beneath; he might be determined to pretend that everything was in his stride but the fear was only buried a short way under the surface.

Spotting a café I decided it was worth a look just in case raiders like me had either missed it or left something behind. None of us had eaten for a long time.

We weren't the first to have found the place and the kitchen had been cleared out of pretty much everything. At least the water was still running so we could drink.

I was just about to tell them we had to move on when Adrien stumbled upon a box of pancake mix at the back of a store cupboard. On the one hand: what sort of lousy café sold ready-mix pancakes? On the other: food.

There was a bottle of gas that I managed to hook up to the stove; it was nearly empty but there was enough to light the hob for as long as we'd need. Within ten minutes we had a pile of pancakes and I was, once again, the biggest hero in all of Paris, at least to these two.

'I used to like them with chocolate spread,' said Adrien as he rolled a pancake up and began to eat it. 'But I think they're even better like this.'

'They're not,' said Gabi, far more honest. She looked at me. 'But I'm glad we have them.'

'Yeah,' I agreed.

Normally I wouldn't have wanted to hang around in the café but I decided that they could both do with a little rest, especially Gabi with her foot. Even once we were back underground and comparatively safe, it would be a long trek before we were home.

I made them both drink plenty of water and filled an empty bottle with more so we'd have some for the journey.

Chapter Fourteen

AFTER HALF AN hour I decided we really did need to move.

I continued to carry Gabi. She said her ankle was feeling better but I could tell from the way she limped on it that it would only get worse if she used it. There would be sections in the tunnels when I wouldn't have space to carry her, best to save her strength for then.

As we continued up the street there was suddenly the most incredible sound. Operatic singing, loud and complicated, the sort of singing that's far more interested in showing off than holding a tune. It climbed up until it hit a note so high it trailed into either silence or a frequency we could no longer hear. A few seconds later there was the shattering of glass.

'Who's that?' Gabi asked. 'She sounds pretty.'

'She sounds shrieky,' said Adrien, 'like someone set fire to a singer.'

'You just don't know what nice music sounds like,' Gabi replied and I felt her legs tense against my neck. Was she really going to have a fight about their different musical tastes? I wasn't sure I could handle that.

'Quiet you two,' I said, 'we don't know it's safe, so better to creep past without them even knowing we're here.'

The singing started again, more convoluted chasing through notes, low to high, like a boxer fighting a tune that was swooping down on them. As we passed the Place de l'Opéra the source of the singing was revealed. A large woman in a bright red evening gown was stood in front of the Palais Garner, arms spread wide as she hurled her voice to the sky.

'Can't we stop and listen to her for a minute?' asked Gabi. 'She's so lovely.'

Adrien rolled his eyes. I have to say I wasn't too struck by her voice either but then—feel free to mock me all you like—I've always hated opera. That wasn't the reason I didn't want to hang around though, I just wanted to keep moving, get underground, get safe.

'We should keep going,' I told her. 'Sorry, but it's dangerous out here in the open.'

'She can't be dangerous,' she replied. 'Not sounding like that.'

'It's not her I'm worried about,' I said, but then, the woman soared for another high note and, almost directly in the line of fire, all three of us cringed as our ears began ringing.

'If she keeps that up,' said Adrien, once the note had dropped lower again, 'she'll blow our heads off.'

'An astute observation,' said a voice from behind us, 'her voice is capable of anything.' My ears were still making a buzzing noise but I turned to face a man dressed in flowing red robes that matched the singer's dress. On his head he wore a red headscarf covered by a wide-brimmed black hat. An enormous red feather swept across the hat's brim. His voice was muffled by the skull mask he wore, an image matched on the head of a long black cane he carried. As soon as Gabi saw him she nearly crushed my neck between her legs. Adrien took a slight step behind me, too worried to pretend he was brave.

The man bowed, his robes and the feather on his hat waving in the wind.

'Greetings my friends, I am Erik, and the delicious voice you are hearing belongs to the legendary Christine Daaé. The Mistress of the Minim, Queen of Crotchets.'

'What's a crotchet?' asked Adrien, rather nervously.

'Putty in her hand, my young friend, putty in her hand. You are privileged to hear her preparing for her comeback performance. Truly, the city is blessed to once more hear her voice.'

'I'm sure,' I agreed, not wanting to get into an argument with the sort of man who wears a mask of a skull. 'When did she last sing?'

'Oh,' Erik replied, adopting a posture of one deep in thought, 'it is so long one can no longer remember. Perhaps she never even did. Not really. It's so hard to be sure.'

Now he adopted a jolly pose, hands on his hips, cane jutting up to one side. All of his movements were slightly over-the-top, as if he were miming the meaning behind everything he said. 'You will, of course, be eager to attend the performance!'

'Well, actually,' I said, 'we'd love to but we've got to be getting home, our friends will be worrying about us.'

I made to move away but he shifted to block me. 'But you can't refuse, surely? How could you bear to live a moment longer knowing you had missed her performance?'

'Maybe we could come back for it?' suggested Adrien, 'and bring our friends. What time does it start?'

I was impressed by his quick thinking and nodded at the idea. 'That would be perfect. It wouldn't take us long to go home and gather everyone together. It would be awful for them to miss it, wouldn't it?'

'But what an awful risk,' he said, 'anything can happen on these streets. They are filled with terrors. If you were to die then you would do so bereft of the grace of her full performance.'

'Which would be terrible,' I agreed, 'but how could we enjoy it knowing that our friends had missed it?'

He thought about this for a moment. 'How many friends do you have?'

'There's a whole colony of us,' I explained, 'over a hundred people.'

He sighed. 'That would be lovely. An audience that might begin to be worthy of her.' He leaned in close. 'I confess I worry that few will turn up. It was always hard to drag the dull masses to the arts. More so now so many of them keep dying and fighting one another. Nothing crushes a performer's spirit more than the ignoble sight of empty seats.'

He thought some more, tapping his cane on the street. Finally, he came to a decision.

'I will trust you,' he said, 'because my love for her

knows no bounds and the idea of a full house swells my heart. Go then, but be back here at eight for the experience of your lives.'

At that moment, Christine Daaé belted out another note that took out a shop window opposite.

Erik clutched his hands to his chest as if to keep his heart in. 'Isn't she the most amazing thing you ever heard?'

'If God could sing,' said Adrien, 'she'd still beat Him I reckon.'

Erik wailed with pleasure, grabbed Adrien and swept him up into a hug. 'You are delicious!' he cried. 'Hurry back with all your friends.'

We left as quickly as we could, waving and grinning and doing our best to appear very much like three people who could be completely and utterly trusted.

'We're not really coming back are we?' Adrien asked.

'Not a chance,' I told him. 'Once we get back to the tunnels I'm not leaving again.'

'That's mean,' Gabi said. 'It'll make him really sad.'

'It would make me really sad having to listen to any more of her noise,' Adrien replied.

'Horrible,' Gabi said and I could sense a tantrum forthcoming.

'We have to think of safety first,' I told her, 'and I'm sure he'll get an audience really. The way she's singing lots of people are bound to turn up aren't they?'

'You're just saying that to make me shut up, you hated her too.'

She had me there.

Chapter Fifteen

WE CUT UP la Fayette and then towards la Victoire. As we emerged across from the synagogue, the air was once-more filled with noise. A chorus of frogs all croaking in the swamp-like world la Victoire had become. The buildings were covered in vines and thick moss, water dripped from the old stone, trickling down the street in a rubbish-filled river. Trees emerged from windows and split wounds in the tarmac of the road. The entire street was a jungle.

'It's beautiful,' said Gabi, her bad mood vanishing at the sight.

Adrien ran ahead, splashing in the shallow water running down the street.

'Be careful!' I told him. It seemed like I was always telling him to be careful.

'It's fine,' he said, chasing after a large grasshopper that had jumped from the leaves of a bush as he'd run towards it.

Fine? Not a word I associated with the city post-Change but I was tired of always telling him off and just kept watch as we walked down the street. He picked up a stick and began poking at the undergrowth as we passed, I hoped nothing lethal poked back.

Above us the frogs continued their music. They were sat on ledges and window sills, filling up every spare inch of horizontal space. It *was* beautiful and I told Gabi so, happy to show I agreed with her. She laughed as a brightly coloured bird burst from the branches of a cypress tree that had rooted itself in the bricks of a mobile-phone store.

'Look at this!' Adrien shouted.

I jogged over to join him. He was looking down at where a large, deep pool had formed in the road. In the water great schools of luminescent fish swirled around in arcs, bands of yellow and green lighting up the dark water.

As we watched, the fish stopped swimming and tilted up towards us. Panicking slightly, I pulled Adrien back as they rose to the surface.

'They're only fish,' he said, pulling away.

'That means nothing,' I told him. 'They could be killer fish.'

One by one, their bright, pointed faces emerged from the water, the surface broken by thirty or more as they stared at us in curiosity.

'See?' Adrien said, moving back to the edge of the water. 'They just want to look at us.'

'It's funny,' said Gabi as I moved back to stand next to Adrien. 'We want to see them because we think they're weird. But to them we're the weird ones and they can't stop staring.'

'Everything's weird,' said Adrien. 'You just have to think about it hard enough to notice sometimes.'

We stood there for a while then began to circle the water; as we moved so did the fish, turning so they continued to face us. Noticing this, Adrien couldn't resist switching directions, then running around the edge so that the fish spun to keep up with him. I was just about to shout for him to be careful when I stopped myself. Just for once I decided to let him enjoy himself without me moaning about it.

Seeing him laugh, just like a normal kid, one that doesn't have to think about monsters on every street, made me almost as happy as he was. After a moment I started running around in the opposite direction, Gabi giggling on my shoulders as she bounced up and down.

The fish separated out into two circles, each turning in an opposite direction so they could follow each of us. That made us laugh even more.

Three people in a stupid world, laughing at something beautiful and strange as, around us, a chorus of frogs grew louder and louder.

Eventually we ran away from the pool, jumping over the creepers and roots along the Rue la Victoire, still laughing, a moment of pure pleasure.

I'm glad of it. It means that, as awful as what happened was, at least they both died happy.

Chapter Sixteen

THE VEGETATION OF la Victoire thinned out as we walked. Once we'd reached Lorette it had vanished altogether.

'One day,' said Adrien, 'the whole of Paris will be like that. All trees and stuff.'

'Good,' said Gabi, 'that would be nice.'

I think she was right. The sooner the city stopped remembering what it *was* and got on with being what it *is* the better we'd all like it.

We'd reached the junction with Saint-Lazare when they attacked. The first we knew of them was the shadows suddenly sweeping across the ground in front of us. Looking up, silhouetted against the sun we saw what cast the shadows. There were two of them, gargoyles set free from their perches at the Notre Dame, their elongated snouts sniffing at the air, their stone mouths snapping open and closed at the prospect of food.

Before I had chance to even think, Gabi was snatched from my shoulders. She kicked out in panic, her heel smacking off the side of my head. For a moment I was disorientated, my vision blurred as I flailed around trying to snatch her back. I felt myself stumble and then I fell on my back in the road, the air knocked from me.

Adrien was screaming and suddenly he flashed past me, held fast in the jaws of the second gargoyle.

I shouted his name and jumped to my feet but the gargoyles were too quick, I ran down the street watching as they became smaller and smaller in the sky, black silhouettes then nothing.

After everything, all it had taken was a few seconds, a moment of shock and I was alone. Both of the kids taken from me.

Chapter Seventeen

I IMAGINE YOU find that funny? After everything I'd done to rescue Adrien and Gabi, after the things we'd faced. Then... BOOM! All over. In seconds. No warning, no foreshadowing, just two kids dead. It had all been a waste of time. A waste.

Two dead kids and me left stood in the middle of the city, alone.

What? You expected a happy ending? Life doesn't do those anymore. Maybe it never did. In life, things are sudden, random, pointless and often heart-breaking.

Get over it.

Although I probably never will.

Chapter Eighteen

STANDING THERE ON Lorette I had no idea what to do. I wondered if it was worth trying to pursue Adrien and Gabi but, really, what would have been the point? There was no way they were still alive and, even if they were, they wouldn't be by the time I got to Notre Dame.

So the only option left was to go home without them.

Except I couldn't be bothered. I just didn't care. The entire reason for the last twenty-four hours or so had just been snatched away. It left me feeling hollow. I think I stood there for about half an hour, just staring into the sky.

When I eventually turned around and carried on walking the way we had been going I was still on automatic, just moving for the sake of it.

Did I cry? I don't remember. I don't think so. I think that would have come once the numbness, the shock had passed. Of course I never had time, I'd only moved a few metres when there was the roar of a van engine and suddenly the air was filled with smoke and a popping like gunfire.

I dropped to my knees.

The smoke rolled down the street, thick, white and odourless. It settled around me until I could barely see.

There was another volley of the popping sound and something shot right past my face and imbedded itself with a hard cracking sound in the bricks of the building behind me. I reached out my fingers and felt a thin line of wire. As I moved, I became aware of others, a whole net of wires. A web.

The smoke was tasteless but had a sweet, nutty odour to it. It made me think of the fairground, of the sputter of theatrical dry ice from machines on the ghost train.

The van engine had stopped and, for a moment the street was utterly silent. Then there came a light, clicking sound, like castanets. As it grew louder, I saw shadows in the thinning smoke. It looked like a line of men marching. Then, as they reached the wires I assumed, they split off and began forming strange, irregular shadows as they ducked and danced around the web. The wires began pinging with a musical sound as they plucked them, drawing closer and closer.

I began to move in the opposite direction.

With every step the wire net seemed to become more complex. Forced to zig-zag my way along, feeling for gaps big enough to pull myself through. The men behind were quicker, their clicking getting louder at every moment.

I turned to look and suddenly a face loomed up out of the smoke. It was the painted, wooden face of a puppet, the clicking sound was its mouth opening and shutting like a decorative nutcracker.

It reached for me and I fell back into the wires, trying to fight it off—though not too hard, I had very little fight left in me. I punched it but all that did was bruise my knuckles. You can't punch wood.

After a few seconds I was surrounded by them, all puppets, all with different designs and costumes. A pirate, a judge, a queen, a cave-woman. They held me down and there was a bright flash and the clicking sound of a camera going off. One of the puppets had a camera for its eye, the flash bursting from its open mouth.

As they dragged me behind them, their wooden fingers

snipping the trapping wires as they passed, I heard the sound of whirring and the camera puppet began producing scrolls of paper from a slit in its belly.

We approached the van, the door was opened and I was thrown inside.

The last thing I saw before the door was closed was the camera puppet pasting one of the sheets he had produced onto the door of a shop. It was a picture of my face beneath a bold announcement: APPEARING SHORTLY AT THE THEATRE DU GRAND GUIGNOL.

Chapter Nineteen

WHICH ALMOST BRINGS us up to date doesn't it? But I've started this story so I'll finish it properly. After all, I know what happens to me when it ends. I'm ready for that. Maybe I'll even welcome it but I'm not rushing this just for you. Out there. Taking pleasure in all this. You'll listen until I finish, I may not have much power here but I still have that.

I lay on the floor of the van, surrounded by the puppets. they swayed as the van took the tight corners, their dead, painted eyes fixed on me.

It was only a couple of minutes before the van pulled up and the doors were opened. They carried me out and I saw the outside of this place, the old theatre, the horror palace, reborn at the centre of Rue Chaptal.

I'd never heard of it before. Why should I? It closed years ago, but as they carried me through the doors and into the dark, velvet-lined foyer I saw the posters on the walls. Severed heads sat in thick red paint, skeletons looming over terrified victims, bizarre creatures with crimson eyes looming towards the reader.

'Ah!' said a voice. 'Perfect. We have our matinee.'

I tried to look but the puppets blocked my view and I was carried back stage and dumped in a threadbare dressing room. The carpet was bald and the cream paint turned bile yellow on the damp walls.

I stood up and saw myself in the dusty mirror fixed on one wall.

It was a face I hadn't paid attention to for a long time, and I had the strange sensation of not quite recognising myself.

As I was staring, a small, elderly man entered. He was dressed in old-fashioned clothes, black britches and dirty stockings. A brown jacket, frayed around the edges just about concealed a shirt splattered with old blood stains. He peered at me over a pair of old, wire glasses. His scalp was flaking and he made a habit of scratching it, the gap beneath his nails crammed thick with wedges of yellow, dead skin.

'Name?' he asked preparing to write on a clipboard.

I didn't bother to answer.

He sighed. 'It's not vitally important of course but it would be useful to have it. Monsieur DuChamp does like these things done properly.'

'Monsieur DuChamp?'

'Current owner of the theatre and international patron of the arts. It is thanks to his kind efforts that we are one more a thriving concern. After being dark for nearly sixty years, the Grand Guignol once more thrills its audiences with the most horrific, most taboo productions the stage has ever seen.'

'Never heard of it.' I enjoyed the appalled look on the old man's face.

'Never heard of it? We are a landmark! A blazing star in the history of theatre. From the last breath of the nineteenth century and well into the twentieth we offered dismemberment nightly. Eyes plucked. Throats cut. Nobody ever knew our methods, the recipe for our stage blood a closely guarded secret. Of course, once the Nazis showed the world what real atrocity looked like we seemed tame by comparison but for thirty years there were no other nightmares as vital as ours. The audience used to pass out you know. Indeed, we used to gauge the success of our little stories by how many could make it out of the stalls on their own two legs!'

He laughed and the skin around his lips split with the effort, a thick, almost black juice seeping from the wound.

'Excuse me,' he said, mopping at the liquid with a stained handkerchief. 'Like noble Paris herself, I am not quite what I used to be.' He folded the handkerchief away. 'Indeed, what is? Even our theatre has changed. I must confess I am not entirely sure what live streaming is but I am assured by Monsieur DuChamp that it is terribly successful. Some of the most noble and wealthy figures on the planet watch our little shows from afar. The magic of the Grand Guignol spreading out across the world.'

'The world's dead,' I told him. 'You might have noticed?'

'Ah!' He smiled, more carefully now, not wanting to split his wound again. 'You are equating the world with its inhabitants. Worlds don't die young man, at least, not so easily as all that. Yes, many died after the unusual events of a few months ago.'

'The Change.'

'Indeed, I believe that is what everyone is calling it. But just because some of the population died that it is not to say the world is empty. Clearly not, the two of us are here are we not?' He scratched at his jacket. 'Accepted, one of us is more "alive" in the scientific sense than the other but I feel we are beyond such shallow viewpoints now, are we not? And, just as there has always been those who rule and those who serve, Monsieur DuChamp and his fellow members of the Hellfire Club have risen to even greater positions of authority. They have divided the planet between them, with agents working in London, New York, Tokyo… and of course Monsieur DuChamp here in Europe.'

'Authority over what?' It seemed beyond stupid. There was nothing left to rule and I told him so.

'Where there is a… now, what was the word Monsieur DuChamp used? Yes… "infrastructure". I believe that was it. There will always be a society. You have electrical power, yes? You have food. You have weaponry. And you have… again the term is somewhat alien to me, "Internet"? You have a population. The world may have changed young man but there will always be those who lead. Monsieur DuChamp is one of those people and the audience, those highly respected souls who take pleasure in our little horror show are others. Put simply, even if the world's population only consisted of two people and a stick, one of those people would be holding the stick and the other would be bowing before him. It is human nature, young man, and let us be thankful for it. Now, what is your name?'

I told him, there seemed little harm in it. I was still thinking of what he'd said. It seemed—seems—utterly ridiculous to me. The Change broke everything and yet there are still some of you out there who insist on trying to maintain the old ways. You think you're superior. You think you're rich. What's rich? Having a full belly and a bed for the night. Anything else is disposable now and the sooner you all remember that the sooner we can get on, fix what's broken and evolve.

But you don't want to, do you? You're happy sitting there in front of your screens, experiencing horror second-hand. Does it really excite you? Hearing my story? hearing about awful things you'll never have to experience, walled away in your pretend homes, your isolated caves?

Who needs evolution when you have easy entertainment?

'So what do I do?' I asked the old man.

'You just tell your story,' he explained, 'the things you saw out there. The monsters you've faced. I imagine you've lost loved ones?'

'Yes,' I said, a wave of anger rising up inside me to have this ghoul so much as mention it.

'Excellent, they'll love hearing about that.'

'And then what?'

'What? After your tale is done? Well, then we offer the final act but you don't have to worry about that. We're terribly skilled you know. Naturally it will be somewhat uncomfortable and protracted—our audience does love to hear the screams—but it won't last forever and then you can rest.'

'Rest? You mean die?'

'Well, in a sense, though this place is filled with the souls of the dead. Nobody ever really dies in theatre after all, you'll be up and about again in time for the evening performance. Our cast grows twice nightly.'

He stood up. 'Now I shall leave you to prepare. Curtain up in an hour. Break a leg, as they say,' he chuckled, 'and if you don't then rest assured, once your tale is done the cast of players will certainly break it for you.'

He left. I waited for a few moments and then moved to the door. To my surprise it wasn't locked so I stepped outside and worked my way back along the corridor. It smelled of damp and rot, old smoke and burned-out furniture.

As I drew close to the foyer I became aware of the clicking sound of the puppets, they stood in a line between me and the exit. Clearly there was no way out that way.

I retraced my steps, thinking there must be a rear exit, a stage door that might be unguarded.

I tried a door opposite the dressing room I had been taken to. This was a larger space; rows of costumes and papier-mâché masks. Mirrors on the walls were cracked and spotted with mould.

At the far end was another door, I tried the handle but it was locked. Just as I was about to leave, the main door opened and I ran and hid behind a rail of costumes as several people filed in. Men and women, all with vacant looks on their faces and tatty clothes that showed they had come from outside. Were these the previous "stars" of DuChamp's new Grand Guignol? If so, for all the dead look in their eyes they were still standing. Perhaps I would survive this after all.

As I watched they began to strip, preparing, I supposed, for this afternoon's performance—*my* performance. Fear gave way to embarrassment, which utterly ridiculous, but as they peeled off their clothes, I felt I had become less a fugitive and more a peeping tom. A man stood right in front of me, his eyes fixed on the wall behind me as his fingers burrowed in the loose skin of his neck. All of a sudden he began to peel. He had been naked but still he stripped further, peeling back skin and muscle to reveal the bone beneath.

The rest of them did the same, flesh falling to the floor as soft, wobbling husks, leaving a room full of wet skeletons, the perfect actors, waiting to try on a new character.

I must have made a noise of shock because, all of a sudden, finger bones were pulling the costumes aside and tugging me out of my hiding place.

They said nothing (how could they? Their lips and tongues lay on the floor alongside the rest of their flesh), just carried me back to my dressing room.

And so I waited, still feeling their wet touch on my cheeks and hands. I stared at my broken face in the mirror and accepted what was to come.

The knock on the door finally came. Outside, one of the puppets, its head a grinning shark, bright white teeth and shining, dead black eyes. It led me out here. Onto this stage.

I can hear the cast moving in the darkness, the creak of the old seats, the shuffle and click of dead bones.

They're waiting for their turn to join me up here. To play out the final act. To show you where my secret zips and buttons lie. To peel away the skin and muscle that makes me who I am.

I can see the red lights of the cameras. And I know you're out there, waiting for me to finish. Waiting for me to die for your pleasure. Well, that time has come. This was the story I had to tell and I've told it.

HE LOWERS HIS head in the spotlight and, all around the world, the remote viewers lean forward wanting to catch every little detail of what is to follow. They will replay it later but there is nothing quite like the thrill of a live transmission, knowing that the screams that echo through the speakers are happening at that very moment.

What will his last expression be? Horror? Fatal acceptance? Tears? They've seen all that and more.

As they press their noses to the screen it is with considerable surprise they note he is smiling.

He looks up, fixes his eyes on the closest camera and speaks once more.

'By the way,' he says, 'I was lying about the gargoyles.'

Chapter Twenty

Later…

WHAT WOULD LOIC do without me, eh? I've always had his back.

'Adrien,' he says, 'if it wasn't for you I'd never make it through the day.'

And, you know what, he's got a point.

It was sad when all the trees and stuff stopped. We'd liked it on la Victoire but that was OK, we were going home and that was the important thing. But then these weird puppets came out of nowhere!

No, not silly little puppets, things on strings, these were proper huge people-sized puppets. In a van. Which was a bit weird. Whatever.

So, anyway, they shot all this smoke and wires at us. The wires were all crossed over in the street and it was really hard to move because wherever you went you touched one and it was hard to move, you know?

We couldn't see, we were all caught up and these huge puppet things were trying to catch us.

Loic was the problem because he was just so big.

'Get out of here,' he said, because he's like that, always trying to be the hero and stuff.

I didn't want to leave him, of course, but I had to think about Gabi too. She's only a girl and she's only eight. No, hang on, don't get all cross, I mean she's only a girl because... well.. oh shut up, let me tell my story ok? Girls are great. Not even a pain or anything. Whatever. God.

So, I had to help Gabi — who's a really *brilliant* girl... better? So I grabbed her and pulled her through the wires. We could move where Loic couldn't, and, with the smoke, the puppet things didn't even see us as we ran off. If puppets can see. Their eyes are made of paint aren't they? Still, The Impressionists are made out of paint too and they could do loads of stuff.

We went back around the corner into La Victoire and hid behind a bush as the puppets picked up Loic and put him in their van. One of them was sticking posters all over the place.

Once the van had driven off we ran over and had a look at one. It had Loic's face on them and said he was appearing at the Theatre du Grand Guignol. Which is a really old theatre that used to show brilliant plays about killing. Didn't you know that? Everyone knows that. No, it's not just because I found out later. I already knew all about it so shut your face.

And stop picking your nose Henri, you're putting me right off.

Where was I?

So, yeah, we knew where they had taken Loic, didn't we? So we'd just have to go and rescue him, wouldn't we? I mean, it's the least we could do after he'd come after us wasn't it? Not that I wouldn't have got Gabi and me out of that mess on my own anyway but that's not the point. He's a mate, he stuck his neck out for us and now it was our turn to do it for him.

'We can't rescue him on our own!' Gabi said, because she was a bit scared.

'We don't have to do it on our own,' I told her, because I'd already come up with a really brilliant plan.

Chapter Twenty-One

IT WAS SEEING the poster that had done it. Thinking about Loic performing in a show.

Gabi said I didn't need to carry her but I did really so it took me longer than I would have liked to get back to the opera house. Though not that long because I'm pretty strong and Gabi's only… well, you know, she's quite small.

'You're early my dears!' shouted the weird skull-faced man. I didn't like him much but that's ok because if there's one thing you learn when you're a kid it's this: it doesn't matter if you like them, what matters is if they like you. And he did. Well, he was only human! Actually he probably wasn't. Doesn't matter though. I had him wrapped around my finger.

'The show doesn't begin for a few more hours,' he said, 'but no doubt you just wanted to guarantee yourselves front row seats. Very wise, very wise indeed.'

The idea of being sat right in front of the mad shouty woman made my bum itch but I didn't say that. This is the other thing you learn as a kid, you don't always say what you think, grown-ups just don't want to hear it. So, you think about what they *would* like to hear and say that instead, throwing in a bit that's useful for yourself.

'I wish that's what it was, Mr Erik,' I told him, 'because you're right, I'd hate to be stuck at the back where I couldn't see properly. But actually we really need your help.'

'Help?' Erik slumped, his shoulders hanging down, he moved in a really funny way, everything was so over the top. 'I wish I could but I'm terribly busy making sure everything's ready for the debut of the century.'

'Well,' I told him, having already thought this through because I'm brilliant, 'actually I think you'll want to help out here because it could get…'

'Christine Daaé,' said Gabi, because she thought I'd forgotten the woman's name but I hadn't so she needn't have bothered. Shut up Gabi! I really hadn't! Who's telling this? You or me?

'Yeah,' I agreed, 'it could help get the wonderful Mrs Daaé the audience she deserves. You won't believe this but, around the corner someone's setting up a show that clashes with yours! They're trying to steal your audience!'

'Nobody would dare!' he said, putting his arm to his forehead as if he'd just got a really bad headache.

'They dare alright,' I said, 'and they're putting up posters everywhere! They've kidnapped our friend and they're forcing him to be in it! So he'll miss your show too! And we won't be able to get our friends because he's the only one who knows the way.'

Erik shook his head. 'Oh... the trauma of a creative life,' he said. 'That it should be such a hardship merely to bring culture to the world.'

'Yeah,' I agreed, 'so I was thinking, maybe you could help us go and put a stop to this other show? Or, even better, you could bring Mrs Daaé with you and she could sing a bit and show them what they're missing! Be a good bit of publicity wouldn't it? I mean, once they've heard her there's no way they'd stay watching the other, really rubbish show is there? They'd be round here like a shot.'

He thought about this, but not for long because it

was a really good plan and it was always going to work wasn't it?

'We shall do as you say,' he said, 'and I'll bring Edgar with me.' He leaned over to us, as if telling us a secret. 'He's my head of security. If it comes to fisticuffs I can certainly hold my own but best to have a bit of back-up, eh?'

He straightened up and gave a high, piercing whistle. A few seconds later, we saw a shape bouncing down the side of one of the buildings. It was short, wearing a top hat and a black cloak. As it came close I realised it was a big monkey, one of those orange ones, you know a rangatang. Yes that is the proper name for them. I know all about monkeys. Stop interrupting.

As if seeing a rangatang in a hat wasn't weird enough, it had one of those old fashioned razors in its hand, you know, the sort that are like a big folding knife? And it had used it to shave all the hair off its face! It looked mental. Thankfully it didn't cut our heads off or anything. It just bowed and then stood next to Erik, waiting to be told what to do.

'I'll just go and have a word with the artist,' he said, 'best you stay here.'

He shuffled off towards the front of the opera house

where the singer was sat on the steps eating a baguette. It was nice when she was doing that because it meant she wasn't making all the noise. Me, Gabi and the rangatang just sort of stared at each other. After a minute Christine Daaé started shouting at Erik. She obviously wasn't much pleased. We couldn't hear what he was saying back but we could see by his movements, all bowing and pleading, that he was trying to keep her onside.

'She sounds like she's trouble,' I said.

'She's an artist,' said Gabi, 'they can have funny moods. It's allowed.'

'She's a pain in my hairy arse,' said the rangatang, which surprised both of us, though I don't know why. I mean, once you've got over the sight of a shaved monkey in a hat what does it matter if it starts speaking? 'He loves her though,' he said, 'so she gets her own way.'

Not this time. He'd obviously managed to convince her that it was a good idea to come with us because both of them walked back from the Opera House and joined us in the street.

I thought I'd best give her a bit of charm.

'Brilliant to meet you, Mrs Daaé,' I said, giving a little bow. 'I'm a big fan.'

Gabi did a sort of snorting thing then so I gave her a dirty look because the last thing we needed was for her to drop us right in it.

'No autographs,' she said, pushing past us and striding off down the street. Basically, she was a bit of a cow.

Once Edgar saw that I was having to carry Gabi, he offered to take over which was brilliant because he slung her over his shoulder and went bouncing all over the place, swinging off the lampposts and jumping on the cars. I'm sure she really loved it too, even if she did do quite a lot of screaming!

You were! You howled all the way!

Anyway, I led them to where we'd been when the puppets showed up. I pointed out the poster.

'The Grand Guignol!' Erik spat, which was a bit stupid as he was wearing a mask, he probably got it all over his face. 'That's not even art! It's an abattoir! A cheap butcher's shop of perversion!'

'All the more reason to get them shut down then,' I said, hoping he wasn't going to turn around and hike it back to the opera. I needn't have worried, I think he was so scared of having dragged Christine this far that there was no way he was going to let her know it might have been a waste of time.

'Quite right!' he said, glancing towards his star. 'We will rescue the poor unfortunates in the audience and restore their faith in beauty.'

Thankfully, Erik knew the way and it wasn't far. We were stood outside the theatre in about ten minutes.

'How do you want to do this?' I asked. 'I mean... they kidnapped Loic so they're obviously not the sort of people you just have a chat with.'

Looking through the door we saw the foyer was filled with those weird puppet men.

Erik turned to Edgar. 'I suggest we just step inside and discuss matters while the rest of them wait out here.'

Edgar grunted his agreement and they both went in.

Christine kept her distance, wandering off down the street to practise her scales; every now and then she smashed a window by belting out a high note.

I wasn't paying too much attention, I was too busy looking through the door to watch Erik and Edgar as they 'discussed matters' with the puppets.

Edgar was leaping from one side of the room to the other, bouncing off the walls and shrieking at the top of his voice while Erik calmly danced among them, swinging his cane and beating them around the head.

The puppets gave a good fight, their wooden arms and

legs flashing to and fro as they tried to defend themselves but they never stood a chance. It was maybe a whole minute before the last one was beaten to splinters by its own arm, torn off by Edgar and used as a club.

Erik popped his head back out and called up the street to Christine. 'Darling? We're all in agreement here so maybe you'd like to accompany us in a meeting with the management?'

She nodded and pushed past us all, insisting on walking in front.

'What's going on?' asked a scruffy old man who had come running, no doubt having heard his puppets being kicked to smithereens. 'Monsieur DuChamp will not tolerate this sort of behaviour.'

'Monsieur DuChamp?' asked Erik.

'The proprietor,' the old man told him, 'and our glorious benefactor.'

Erik nodded. 'Would you be so good as to explain to Monsieur DuChamp that we would very much like a few moments of his time.'

'That's quite impossible,' the old man said, 'he's not here. I am the manager here and I deal with him exclusively via...' he seemed confused. 'Well, it's sort of like a telephone but you can see the other person's face—and a very noble face it is too—I believe it is known as Skype.'

'Then might I suggest you engage this "Skype" so that we can discuss my star's needs in the same manner?' said Erik.

'I have no intention of disturbing him,' the old man replied, 'he is currently enjoying our matinée and will brook no interruption, certainly not at the request of a lunatic in a mask and his fat girlfriend.'

Which was not the right thing to say. Christine towered over him and, even as he puffed himself up to argue, she bent down and sung a note into his ear. It had an immediate effect, his face turned bright red, his body shook getting more and more violent and then, all of a sudden, he just burst! I know! Sick right? He actually burst! It was like he'd been pumped full of air or something! One of his eyes actually exploded off the wall! It was the best thing ever!

Of course, it also kind of meant that the time for chatting was over, I mean, you blow the management's head off and that's the end of the conversation, yeah?

We walked through to the main auditorium and I could see Loic stood on the stage. He was lit by a single spotlight, he looked beaten and miserable.

'I can see the red lights of the cameras,' he said. 'And I know you're out there, waiting for me to finish. Waiting for me to die for your pleasure. Well, that time has come. This was the story I had to tell and I've told it.'

Then he looked up and saw us stood at the back of the room. He smiled. Then said something that made no sense at all to me until he explained later. 'I didn't want them to come looking for you,' he told me, 'so I'd lied during my story, I made them think you and Gabi were dead.'

But, at the time, he just said, 'I was lying about the gargoyles,' and I thought, *Ok, Loic's gone off his head.*

The room was dark but we could tell there were things shuffling in the rows of seats. Christine pushed past me and made her way up to the stage, ignoring the things that were twitching on either side.

She stood next to Loic and turned back to face us.

'Not much of an audience,' she said, 'and this place stinks.'

'The real audience is out there,' said Loic, pointing up towards the ceiling. 'They're watching from miles away, important people, at least that's what they think. But really they're just stupid, horrible cowards who like seeing people hurt. Bullies.'

'Then we should give them a show,' said Christine.

The audience began to move, rushing towards the stage as if they meant to attack Christine and Loic. I guess that's exactly what they meant to do actually. At the time I was just stood there freaking out at the sight of the things. They were skeletons, the few lights shining off their wet bones as they climbed over the backs of the seats, and made to attack.

Of course, Edgar and Erik weren't going to just stand back and let that happen.

They dived in, Edgar pulling the things apart as he bounded across the rows. He snatched a leg bone from one and used it to smash others to pieces. Erik hardly had to do anything, he just walked down the central aisle, occasionally ducking as a skull was thrown past him. Every now and then he would swing his cane and help out, but Edgar did most of it. That rangatang had a real skill for tearing stuff up. It took next to no time before we were stood in the middle of a broken theatre, crunching our way over snapped bones.

As we gathered on the stage a voice came out of the speakers.

'Well, that was an annoying way to end a perfectly good bit of fun,' it said.

'Would this be Monsieur DuChamp?' asked Erik.

'Yes, it would you bone-faced freak,' said the voice. 'A man that will take considerable pleasure in paying someone to have you and your ugly wife shot at the earliest opportunity.'

'Oh dear,' said Erik, glancing towards Christine. 'I am afraid you may have angered Madame Daaé, a woman I would be blessed to call my betrothed, naturally, though is in fact, merely by guiding light, my shining beauty, my...'

'Oh shut up and go away,' said the voice. 'I have far more important things to do than listen to you for a moment longer.'

'Pray just attend us a few seconds more,' said Erik, gesturing for the rest of us to make for the door. 'I think you'll be amazed when you hear what Madame Daaé has to contribute. She is, after all, the major attraction in the entire country, if not the world...'

'Really?' DuChamp laughed. 'That I would like to hear!'

He was saying it in that annoying way adults have of meaning the complete opposite to what they're saying *but making it really obvious*. Never got that, it's just pointless and annoying.

Erik rushed off the stage, pushing all of us in front of him. We ran out of the room as Christine moved to centre stage, stretching her arms out in the beam of the spot light.

'Run like your heads depend on it!' Erik said as we belted our way through the foyer and out into the street. Having seen what she could do I could imagine our heads really did depend on it so I did as I was told.

There was this building noise as Christine ran through a scale of notes, getting higher and higher and then, even from outside we had to cover our ears as a single loud note bashed its way out of her mouth and appeared to take out the front part of the building. I mean, when your singing can knock down walls you know you've got talent, I'll give her that.

I've no idea what DuChamp made of it but I like to think his head blew up just like the old man's had. Sat miles away, being all smug and annoying then POW! Brains all over the wall. Brilliant.

And that's it. The brilliant story of how I saved Loic (after he might have saved me a little bit).

Of course that's it, that's how you finish stories! With big explosions!

Well, no, some stuff happened afterwards but nothing

really brilliant. Christine came out, she was fine. We convinced her and Erik that we would get a bunch of people together and listen to her sing properly but you know about that don't you? Some of you were there, all bored like me, at the la la la…

She didn't even blow anyone's head off or anything, she just sang. BORING.

Obviously we got back safely, I'm here aren't I? Stupid to tell you that. Like bothering to tell you I've got legs when you can see them with your own eyes.

The point is: we went out there, did some brilliant stuff, were really clever and then came home again. What do you want from me? Blood?

I suppose I could tell you about what happened on the food run last week—yeah of course Loic lets me go on the food runs now, he needs me to watch his back, obviously—that was pretty good. I didn't know pirañas could fly… Eh? Oh. Paulette says we haven't got time because you all need to go to bed, sorry, maybe another day. It's a pretty good story, a man has his legs eaten while running along the Champs Elysees… Yeah, yeah, fine Paulette, bed, whatever.

* * *

ADRIEN GETS UP *and leaves Paulette to tuck the kids up and put them to bed.*

In the doorway, Loic is waiting for him, a big smile on his face.

'My hero,' *Loic says.*

'Yeah well,' *Adrien shrugs,* 'you've got to big it up a bit when you're telling a story don't you?'

'You do,' *Loic agrees and they both walk off to get on with the rest of their lives.*

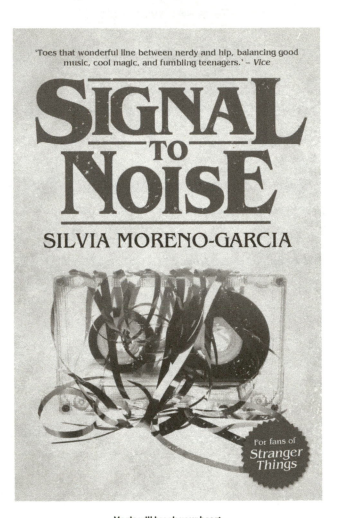

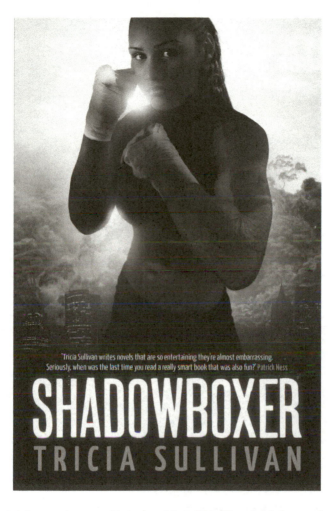

'Tricia Sullivan writes novels that are so entertaining they're almost embarrassing.
Seriously, when was the last time you read a really smart book that was also fun?' Patrick Ness

SHADOWBOXER
TRICIA SULLIVAN

Jade is a seventeen-year-old mixed martial arts fighter. When she's in the cage she
dominates her opponents—but in real life she's out of control.

After she has a confrontation with a Hollywood martial arts star that threatens her gym's
reputation, Jade's coach sends her to a training camp in Thailand for an attitude adjustment.

Hoping to discover herself, she instead uncovers a shocking conspiracy. In a world just
beyond our own, a man is stealing the souls of children to try and live forever.

 WWW.SOLARISBOOKS.COM

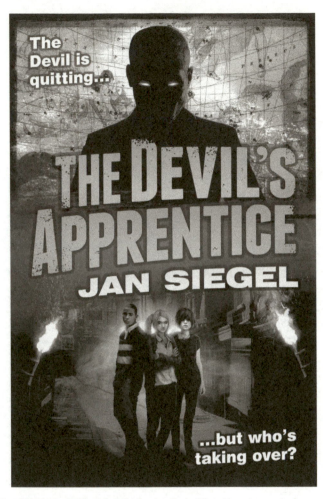

The Devil is quitting...

THE DEVIL'S APPRENTICE

JAN SIEGEL

...but who's taking over?

When Pen inherits the job of caretaker for a London building with no doors and only a secret entrance from the caretaker's lodge – which she must never use – little does she know it will lead her into unbelievable danger. For Azmordis, also known as Satan, a spirit as old as Time and as powerful as the Dark, immortality is running out.

In the house with no front door, a group of teenagers are trapped in assorted dimensions of myth and history, undergoing the trials that will shape them to step into his cloven footwear – or destroy them. Assisted by an aspiring teenage chef called Gavin and Jinx, a young witch with more face-piercing than fae-power, Pen must try to stop the Devil's deadly game – before it's too late.

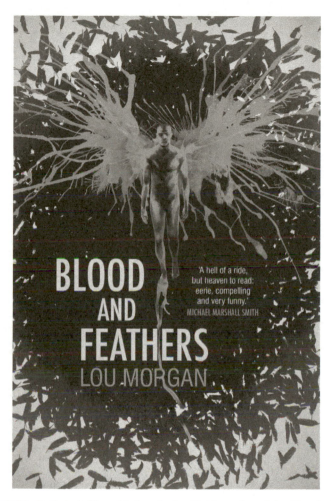

BLOOD AND FEATHERS

LOU MORGAN

'A hell of a ride, but heaven to read: eerie, compelling and very funny.'
MICHAEL MARSHALL SMITH

Alice isn't having the best of days – late for work, missed her bus, and now she's getting rained on – but it's about to get worse.

The war between the angels and the Fallen is escalating and innocent civilians are getting caught in the cross-fire. If the balance is to be restored, the angels must act – or risk the Fallen taking control. Forever. That's where Alice comes in. Hunted by the Fallen and guided by Mallory – a disgraced angel with a drinking problem he doesn't want to fix – Alice will learn the truth about her own history... and why the angels want to send her to hell.

What do the Fallen want from her? How does Mallory know so much about her past? What is it the angels are hiding – and can she trust either side?